LITTLE WALRUS WARNING

SMITHSONIAN OCEANIC COLLECTION

To my husband, Skip Crane
  — C.Y.

To my wife, Pamela, and my children, Erin and Lauren
  — W.S.

Published by Soundprints, an imprint of Trudy Corporation, Norwalk, Connecticut.

Book design: Shields & Partners, Westport, CT

First Paperback Edition 2002
10 9 8 7 6 5 4 3
Printed in Indonesia

Acknowledgments:
    Our very special thanks to the late Dr. Charles Handley of the Department of Vertebrate Zoology
at the Smithsonian Institution's National Museum of Natural History for his curatorial review.

ISBN 1-56899-937-2 (pbk.)

The Library of Congress Cataloging-in-Publication Data below applies only to the hardcover edition of this book.

Library of Congress Cataloging-in-Publication Data

Young, Carol

Little walrus warning / by Carol Young; illustrated by Walter Stuart.
        p.   cm.
Summary: In Alaska a walrus calf and his mother make their last trip together to the summer feeding grounds in the Chukchi Sea before he is ready to leave the nursery herd and take his place with the bulls.
        ISBN 1-56899-271-8
1. Walruses—Juvenile fiction. [1. Walruses—Fiction.]
I. Stuart, Walter, ill. II. Title.
        PZ10.3.Y857Li 1996   95-46201
        [E]—dc20   CIP
                                                                              AC

LITTLE WALRUS WARNING

by Carol Young   Illustrated by Walter Stuart

Soundprints
Where Children Discover...

4

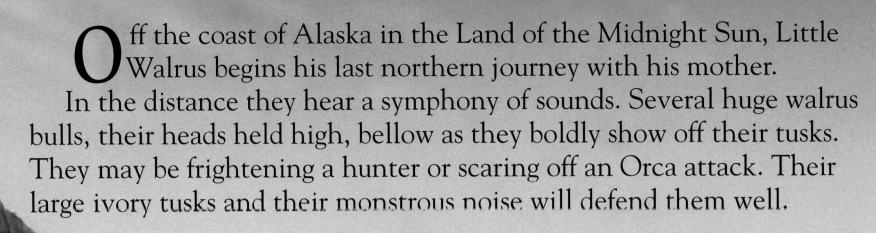

Off the coast of Alaska in the Land of the Midnight Sun, Little Walrus begins his last northern journey with his mother.

In the distance they hear a symphony of sounds. Several huge walrus bulls, their heads held high, bellow as they boldly show off their tusks. They may be frightening a hunter or scaring off an Orca attack. Their large ivory tusks and their monstrous noise will defend them well.

The four-year-old calf has tusks that are not fully grown.
For now he still needs his mother. Leaving the bulls behind
in the spring, they will travel north with the nursery herd.
Sometimes swimming, sometimes hitching rides on giant ice
islands, they will journey hundreds of miles for summer feasting
in the Chukchi Sea.

As cold Arctic winds blow, the cow and her calf haul out of the water onto a floating island of ice. They use their tusks like ice picks and ease the climb up with their flippers.

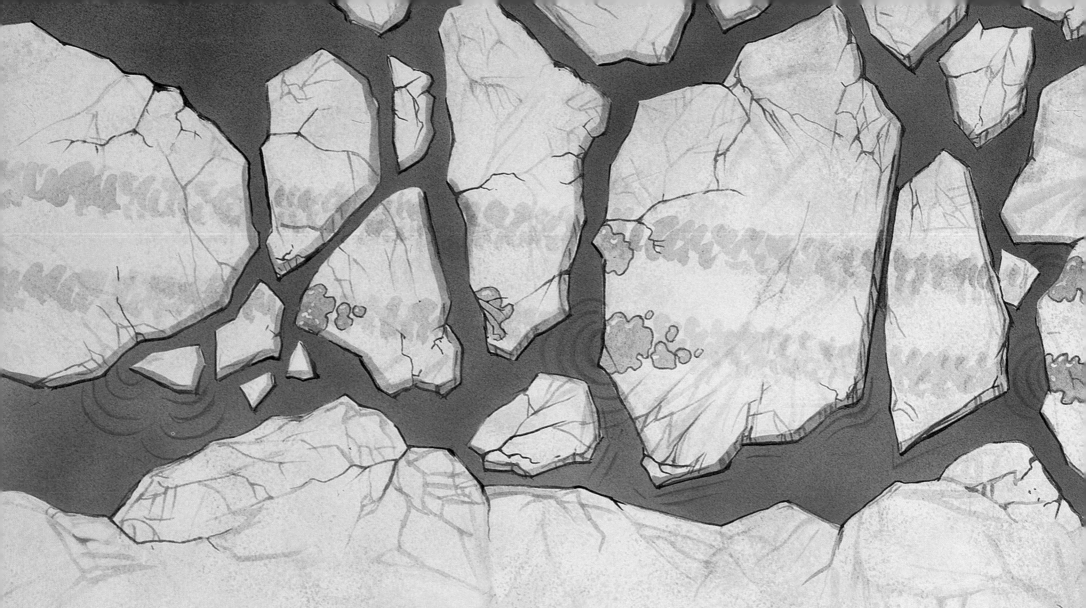

Mother moves across the ice, stabbing it with her tusks now and then to steady herself.

Little Walrus lags further and further behind. Slipping and sliding, he falls between giant wedges of ice.

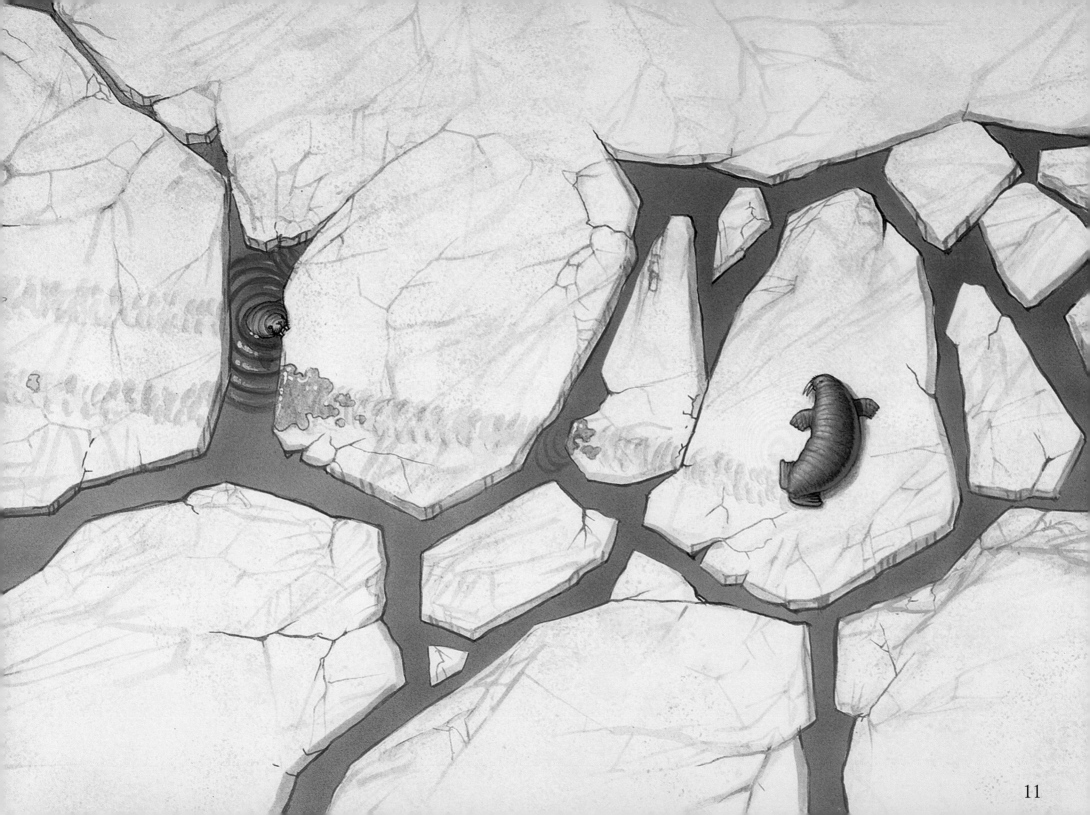

Hearing his pitiful cry, Mother struggles to find Little Walrus. Chips fly as she frantically hacks at the ice. She could break a tusk or fall in the ice trap herself, but it does not matter—what matters is her calf. Frozen chunks shift and groan as her tusks break more and more ice. Steadily, she opens a way of escape and helps Little Walrus to safety.

Mother keeps a close eye on her calf as they continue north, but even on a calm sunny day there can be danger with ice. Surrounded by many walruses, they bask in the late spring sun. Joining the crowd on the same chunk of ice come two, then five, then ten more walruses.

WHOOOOAAA!
These huge walruses are heavy!
The ice chunk tips on its side and
WHOOOOOOOOOOSH!
All of the cows and calves are dumped into the sea.

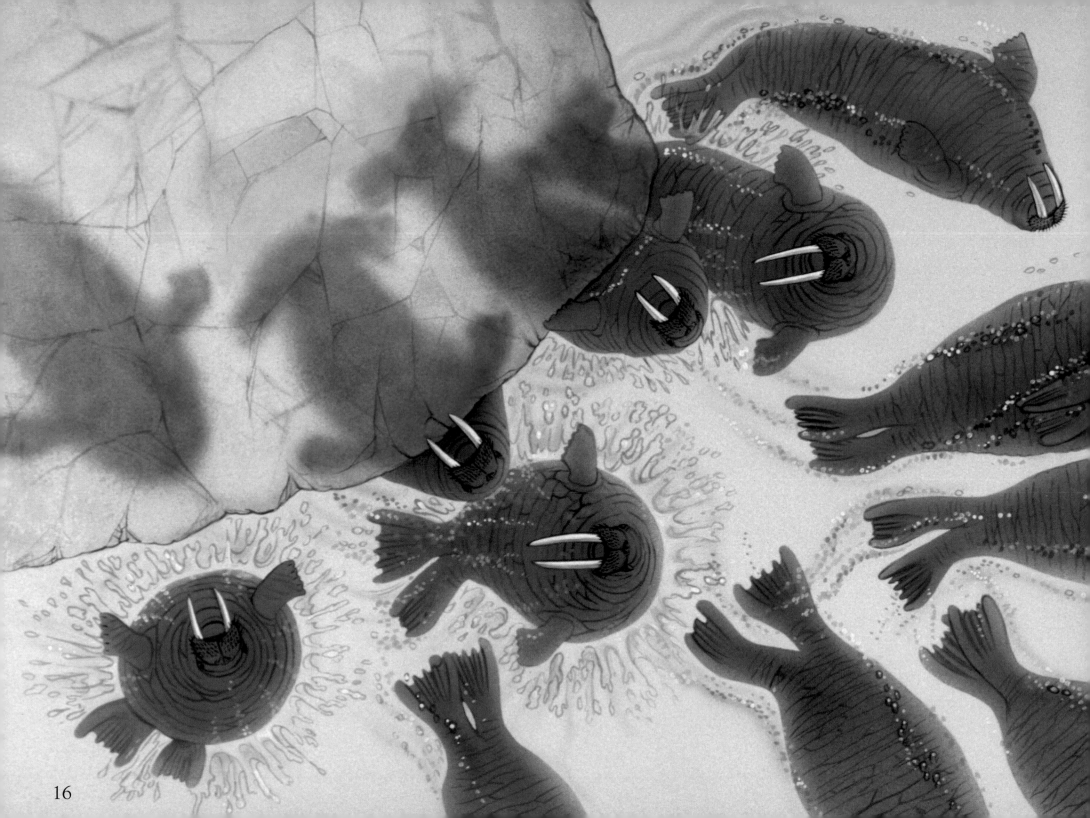

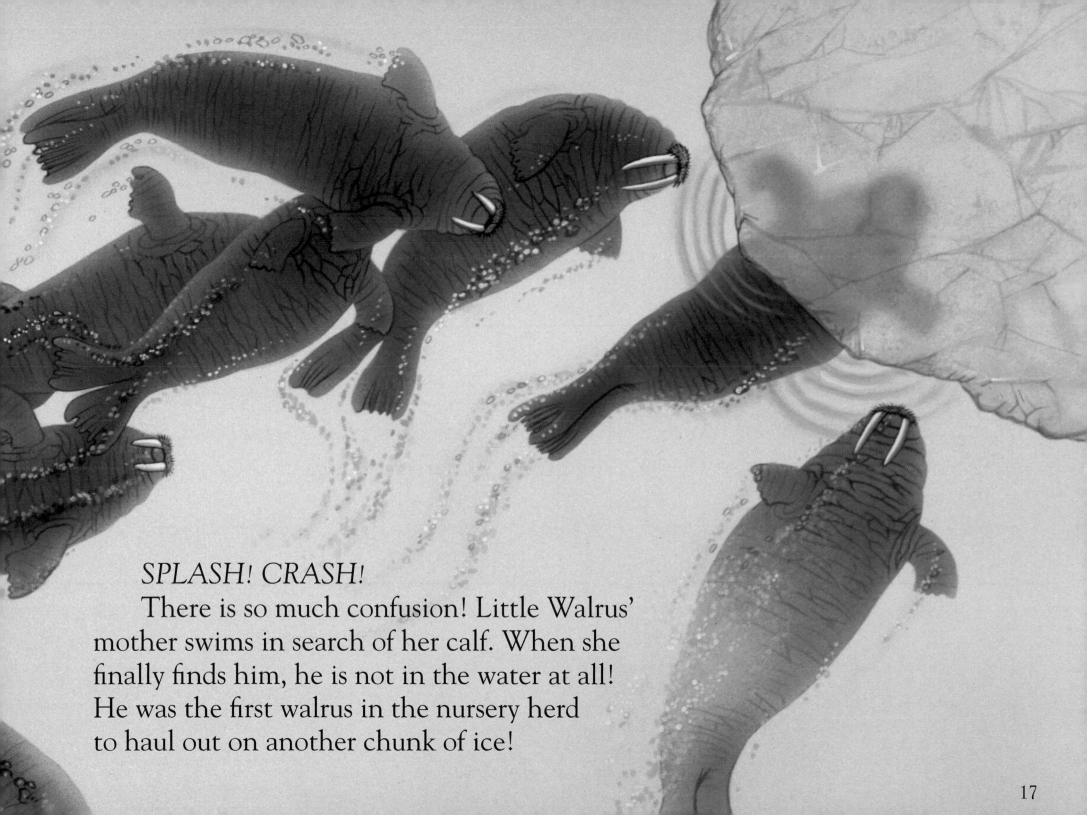

SPLASH! CRASH!
There is so much confusion! Little Walrus'
mother swims in search of her calf. When she
finally finds him, he is not in the water at all!
He was the first walrus in the nursery herd
to haul out on another chunk of ice!

As summer arrives, the herd reaches the rich feeding grounds of the Chukchi Sea. Ice drifts and sparkles under the sun. Here among seals and whales, Little Walrus must master the skills of hunting.

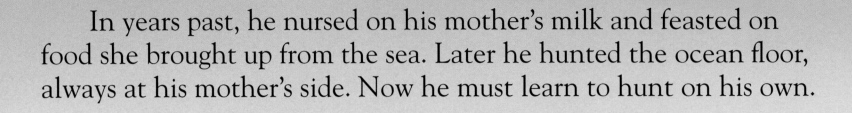

In years past, he nursed on his mother's milk and feasted on food she brought up from the sea. Later he hunted the ocean floor, always at his mother's side. Now he must learn to hunt on his own.

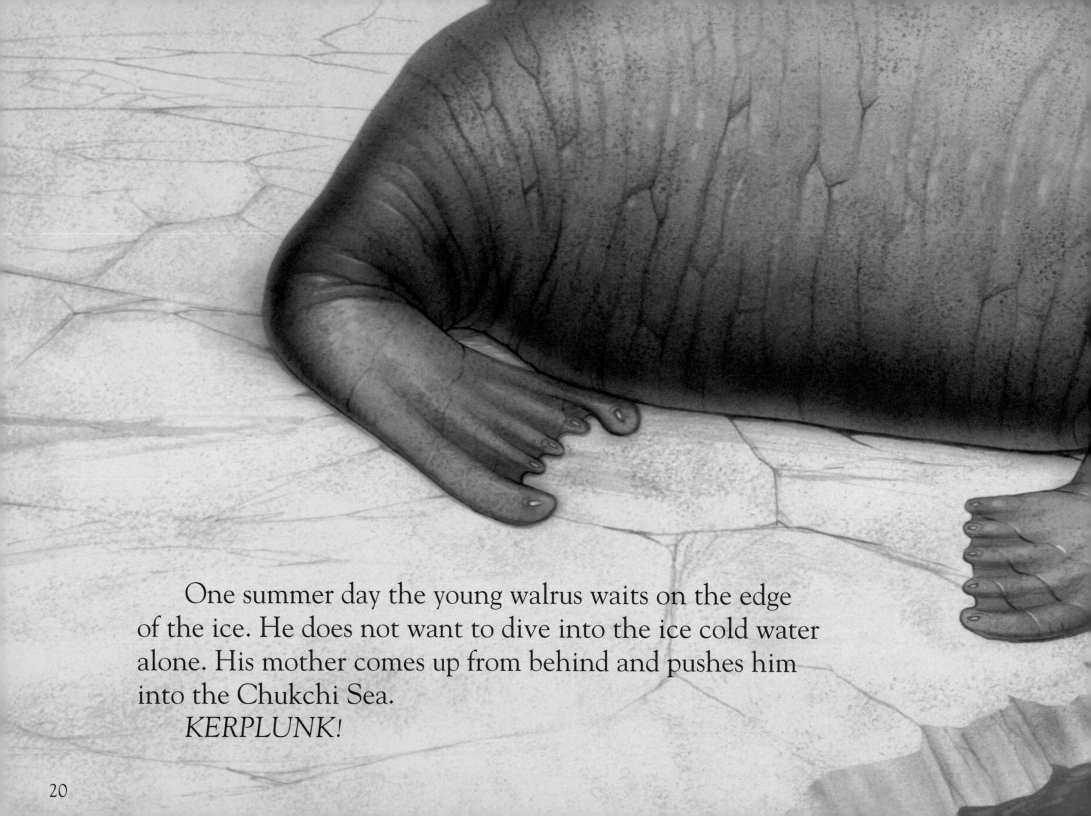

One summer day the young walrus waits on the edge
of the ice. He does not want to dive into the ice cold water
alone. His mother comes up from behind and pushes him
into the Chukchi Sea.
KERPLUNK!

Alone in the water, Little Walrus sinks to the ocean floor to hunt on his own. But the water is murky and muddy along the bottom, and he cannot see any food at all! Little Walrus must use his stiff bristle whiskers to feel in the dark for his food—snails, worms and crabs. He sucks live clams right out of their shells—and swallows them whole.

Full from his feast, he rejoins the herd on the ice.
He circles the huge pile of walruses who are warming
themselves to various shades of pink, red and brown.
He wanders around the edge of the crowd looking for
a spot to lie down.

He does not see the enemy ahead, for the animal is the color of ice and snow. But, sniffing the wind, he smells danger. He lifts his head and thrusts his tusks high in the sky. Little Walrus lets out a *ROAR*—a warning for all to hear!

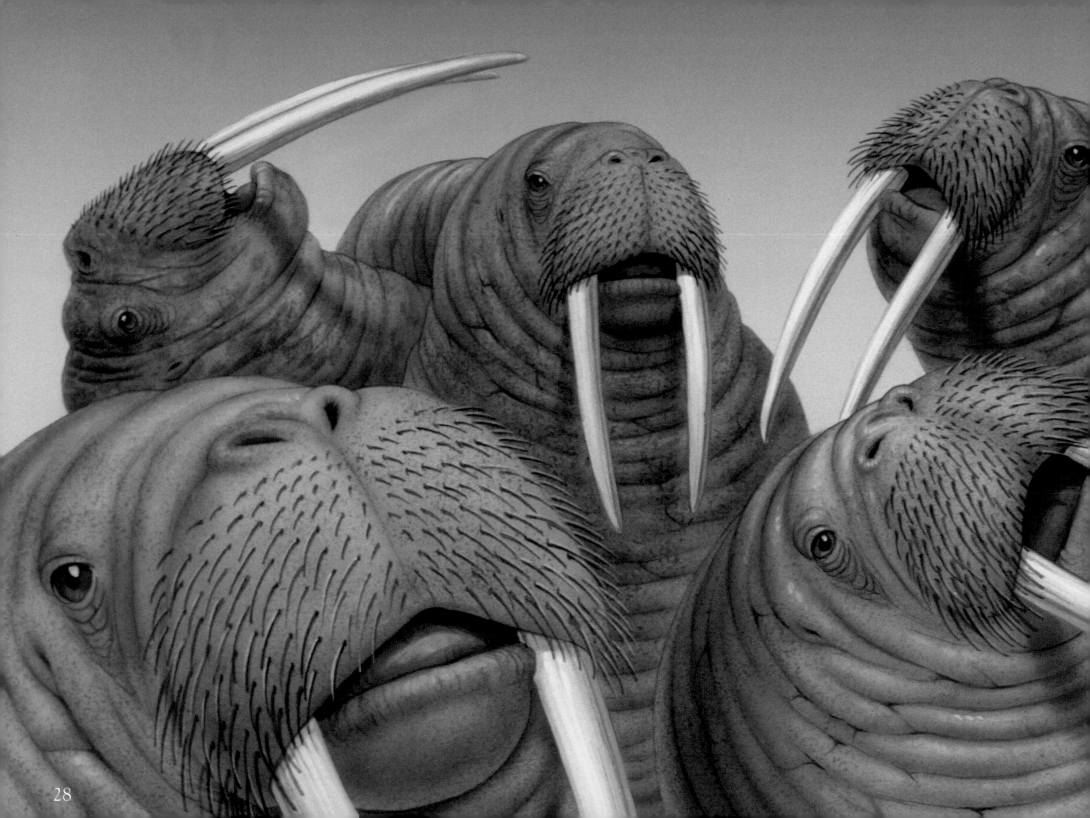

The cows grunt and growl. The calves bark and cry. Their monstrous sounds and the sight of so many gleaming white tusks frighten the creature away. The polar bear retreats into the landscape of snow and ice to search for an easier meal.

Days grow shorter, colder and darker. As islands of ice start to freeze together, the nursery herd heads south for the winter. Following the route of the drifting ice, their journey will end where it began.

Off the coast of the Land of the Midnight Sun the walruses reunite—bulls and cows and all the young. Little Walrus will not go north with the herd next year. He is ready to take his place with the bulls.

About the Walrus

Walruses are highly social and sometimes form herds of as many as several thousand animals. They live in the northern polar regions of the Pacific and Atlantic oceans. A thick layer of blubber keeps them warm in these icy waters.

Most walruses migrate. Calves and cows travel north each spring in search of rich feeding grounds. While many of the bulls migrate as well, they do not travel as far as the others. Walruses can swim as fast as twenty-two miles per hour and dive to depths of over 150 feet.

The walrus' distinctive tusks are actually canine teeth and can grow over 3 feet long for males and 2-1/2 feet long for females. They are used in combat between animals, to "haul out" from the water onto ice, for hooking into the ice to stabilize while sleeping in the water, and for defense against predators.

The walrus' natural enemies are polar bears and orca whales. They are considered a threatened species, primarily due to hunting by humans.

Glossary

bull: an adult male walrus.

calf: a young male or female walrus.

Chukchi Sea: a body of water northwest of Alaska.

cow: an adult female walrus.

flippers: broad, flat limbs adapted for swimming and for walking on land or ice.

haul out: the way a walrus pulls itself out of the water by hooking its tusks on the ice and then using its flippers to help pull itself up.

ivory: the hard creamy-colored portion of a walrus tusk that is highly valued by humans.

Land of the Midnight Sun: Arctic and Antarctic areas where, in summer, the sun does not set. It can still be seen at midnight.

nursery herd: a group of cows and calves.

orca: killer whale.

tusks: the canine teeth of a walrus, which are greatly enlarged in adults.

Points of Interest in this Book

pp. 4-5: orca whale.

pp. 4-5, 30-31: the cliffs of the coastline of Alaska can tower over a thousand feet and are often more jagged than they appear here. Over time, they have been chiselled to sharp angles and edges by ice and frost.

pp. 6-11, 14-17, 20-21, 24-27: ice floes…floating ice that is formed when the surface of the water freezes and pieces are broken off.

pp. 14-15, 18-19: icebergs…floating ice chunks that break off of glaciers as they meet the sea. Icebergs are much larger than they seem—the majority of their mass is hidden beneath the water.

pp. 4-5, 24-25, 30-31: walruses sleep and sunbathe in large groups, preferring the safety of numbers.